This book belongs to:

_____

by: Deb Venable

illustrations by: Elizabeth Ptack

What color is your hair?

What color are your eyes?

What color are you inside?

When you pick your friends,
close your eyes and think.

Is their heart dark gray,
or is it rosy pink?

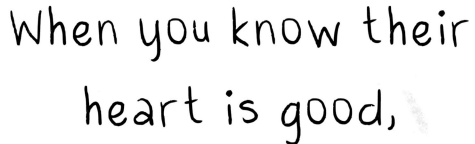

When you know their heart is good,

hug them nice and tight.

They'll be your friend
throughout life

and help every day be bright.

Use this little trick

from the very start.

What really matters most of all...

is the color of your heart.

Dedicated to:
Scott, VJ, Josh and Zach

Special thanks to Britt Spread

Keep living with rosy pink hearts!